DETECTIVE BROTHER

Jamie's Amazing Cape Adventures

First American Edition 2018
Kane Miller, A Division of EDC Publishing

Text © Pete Johnson, 2011
Illustrations © Mike Philips, 2011
The moral rights of the author and illustrator have been asserted.
Published by arrangement with Catnip Publishing Limited, London.

For information contact:
Kane Miller, A Division of EDC Publishing
P.O. Box 470663
Tulsa, OK 74147-0663
www.kanemiller.com
www.edcpub.com
www.usbornebooksandmore.com

Library of Congress Control Number: 2017953606

Printed in the United States of America
1 2 3 4 5 6 7 8 9 10

ISBN: 978-1-61067-744-8

A
Jamie's
Amazing Cape
Adventure

DETECTIVE BROTHER

Pete Johnson
Illustrated by Mike Philips

Kane Miller
A DIVISION OF EDC PUBLISHING

Contents

1. Sharing a Room
with Harry

"I win," shouted Harry, rushing past me.

He charged into the hotel room and jumped onto the bed so heavily it shook.

Then Harry started jumping up and down. "I'm having this bed, Jamie, because it's the best one!" he yelled. Then he added again, "I won."

I shook my head. "You haven't won anything because I wasn't racing you.

And anyway, both the beds in here are exactly the same."

"No, they're not, mine's decent. Your bed is garbage," shrieked Harry. Then he started laughing madly.

I was really happy when Mom told me I was going to have an extra vacation – a few days by the sea to help me get over a really bad case of the flu. And my best friend, Reema, could come too. Excellent! Until I found out that my younger brother, Harry, whom I'd caught the flu from in the first place, would be coming along as well. And, most terrible of all, I was going to have to share a room with him.

Harry, who is the most ANNOYING brother in the whole world. How would I stand it?

I started unpacking, while Harry lay on the bed with his shoes on, singing loudly and totally out of tune.

"You're giving me a headache," I moaned.

"Everyone says I've got a great singing voice," replied Harry.

"No, they don't."

There was a tap on the door and Aunt Nora, who was supposed to be looking after us, came in. Aunt Nora is actually my mom's aunt, so she's incredibly ancient. She means well, but she's very absentminded.

"How's the unpacking coming along?" she asked, with one of her bright smiles.

"I've nearly finished," I said, "but Harry hasn't even started yet. He's too busy trying to sing, except he can't."

"Yes, I can," cried Harry. "Listen to this, Aunt Nora."

"Not right now, dear," said Aunt Nora hastily raising a hand. "And don't sit on the bed with your shoes on. Now hurry up, tea will be ready for us downstairs in five minutes."

Just the mention of food sent Harry leaping to his feet. "Will it include sandwiches and cake?"

"I'm sure it will," said Aunt Nora, smiling at him. "Now I want you two boys to really try and get along. We don't want to spoil this vacation with any arguing, do we?"

"But I never, *ever* start any of the fights," said Harry. "It's always Jamie's fault."

"What?" I cried indignantly.

"I'm sure with a little effort we can all have a really lovely time," said Aunt Nora. "Now I'm just off to tell dear Reema to come down to tea."

After Aunt Nora had gone I had just one more thing to unpack. And I'd left my most special and valuable and most wonderful possession till last.

My cape.

It's dark blue with bright-gold stars around the sides. I found it lying in the branches of a tree. Then

one day I discovered its amazing secret.

My cape can grant wishes too.

You can imagine how totally exciting that is. But lately I've gone a bit wild. And I've asked for too many wishes. I admit that.

And some of the wishes have gone a bit wrong. Like when I wished for a bar of chocolate, just one little square arrived and banged me right in the face.

Sometimes the wishes haven't even come true.

My cape doesn't look as bright and sparkling as it used to either. Reema thinks it's gotten tired and needs a good rest.

Yes, she knows about the cape's magic powers. Unfortunately, so does one other person. That's right – Harry.

I said to him, "You're not allowed to use my magic cape on this vacation. It's got to have a complete rest."

"Have you broken it?" he demanded.

"No, but it needs a break. So leave it alone."

Harry didn't answer.

"Do you understand?" I shouted.

"Stop telling me what to do," said Harry. "You're worse than a teacher."

"I was just . . ."

"Not listening to you," shouted Harry, running out onto the balcony.

I raced after him. But then I forgot all about Harry being a pain. For our hotel was right on the seafront and the view was amazing. I gazed down at the beach and the sea sparkling in the sunlight. I took a

gulp of air. It felt really fresh and strong.
I was about to take a second gulp when I
noticed something very strange.

Silence!

Suddenly Harry had disappeared and
he wasn't making a sound. What was he
up to?

I stepped back inside the room. "Harry," I cried. "Where are you?"

"In the bathroom," he replied, then giggled and came out. He was holding the biggest ice cream cone you've ever seen.

2. An Argument and a Fight

"That ice cream," I cried, pointing at it. It was so huge it nearly hid Harry's face. And there were chocolate bars sticking out of the top. "You wished for it on my cape."

"That's right," said Harry smugly, waving the cape in the air. It was dripping with water, since my cape only works when it's wet.

"But it's *my* cape, and I told you not to touch it," I said.

"I know. That's why I did it," said Harry, a grin all over his silly face. Then he added, "But the cape's working again now. You can get ice cream too." And he threw the cape at me.

I grabbed it quickly and then put my hand on the most magic part of the cape, where the number seven is. I felt a tiny tingling in my hands. "Number Seven, please magic me an ice cream cone that's even bigger than Harry's." Then I waited and waited ... and absolutely nothing happened.

"You've used up all the magic," I said accusingly.

"Ha-ha," said Harry jubilantly. And then he started to laugh. Only it was more of a mean cackle. It was the cackling that got me really mad.

"Give me that ice cream," I demanded, rushing toward Harry.

Well, Harry gave me the ice cream all right – smack in my face.

I let out a roar of fury and soon Harry and I were having this crazy fight, yelling and shouting at each other. I don't know what would have happened if Aunt Nora hadn't burst into the room, closely followed by Reema.

"Stop!" Aunt Nora shrieked. "Stop this at once and get up, both of you."

Harry and I rose sheepishly to our feet, our faces and clothes both smeared with ice cream.

"Honestly, Jamie, I thought you were a nice, sensible boy," said Aunt Nora. "Instead, you're acting like a three year old. I expected you to set a better example for your younger brother."

"Yeah," sniggered Harry. "Naughty Jamie."

I glared at him.

"If you carry on acting like this, I shall move my bed in here," said Aunt Nora.

Both Harry and I gulped in horror.

"You wouldn't," said Harry, his voice shaking.

"I would," said Aunt Nora. "So now clean yourselves up and come downstairs." Then she smiled at Reema, who was hovering in the doorway. "Sorry you had to see this, dear."

I couldn't bear to look at Harry after that. I quickly cleaned myself up.

"Never touch my magic cape again, Harry," I snarled. "Never in your whole life."

"Don't want to," he snapped. "I'm going to do something *much* more exciting."

He waited for me to ask him what that was. But I didn't. I just glared fiercely around the room.

"Come on," Reema whispered to me. "Don't get into another argument."

So we walked off, leaving Harry on his own. And Reema laughed and joked and really cheered me up.

Reema has been my best friend for ages now. And maybe you think it's a bit strange having a girl for a best friend, but I don't. And I was really pleased she was at Seaview with us. Seaview was the name of our hotel.

Aunt Nora was waiting for us downstairs with a tray of tea, sandwiches and cake. "Not that you deserve all this lovely food, Jamie," she said. "But you have been ill and your dear mom did tell me to feed you up." Then she smiled and said, "Well, what are you waiting for, tuck in!" That was one of the great things about Aunt Nora; she was never in a bad mood for long.

Harry came downstairs soon afterward. He was holding a book that told you how to be a detective. He grabbed three pieces of cake, put them all in his mouth at once and started telling Aunt Nora how he was going to spend this vacation solving mysteries, just like a real detective. Crumbs spilled everywhere as he talked, but luckily Aunt Nora is nearsighted and didn't notice.

"I've got a magnifying glass and special gloves, and a beard so I can disguise myself."

I started to laugh. "Harry – the world's worst detective."

"You take that back," said Harry, "or I'll punch you in the face."

"Don't start fighting again," said Aunt Nora wearily. Then she closed her eyes.

"I'm not sleeping, just resting my eyes," she announced. But a few seconds later she started snoring loudly.

Reema giggled and I whispered, "Shall we go and explore the beach?"

"Oh, yes," said Reema eagerly.

"Can I come?" asked Harry.

"No," I snapped. "I've had enough of you for one day."

"Doesn't bother me," said Harry. "I'm going to find myself a mystery to solve." And he marched off.

"He won't find any mysteries here," I said, as Reema and I half ran to the beach.

I told Reema what Harry and I had been arguing about upstairs. "The cape granted Harry's wish, but not mine, which was extremely annoying," I said.

"Try it again now," said Reema, "and don't ask for anything too much."

So I flicked some seawater onto the cape and then wished for one ordinary little ice cream cone.

But nothing happened.

"Like I said," whispered Reema, "your cape probably just needs a good rest. Then it'll be back to granting wishes again."

Before I could reply, a terrible cry rang out. The sound seemed to fill the air.

"Where did that come from?" asked Reema.

I pointed to a seagull on the cliffs above us. It was squawking very loudly and pecking furiously at its feathers.

"The poor thing's really upset about something," said Reema. "But what?"

3. Harry the Dinosaur

We edged closer to the seagull. The bird seemed to be very unhappy. It was letting out these loud, miserable cries. Then I noticed its feathers. They should have been white, but they weren't anymore.

"Look!" I cried. "It's covered in oil."

"Oh, but that's awful."

"And now it's trying to peck the oil off its feathers," I said.

"But it'll poison itself," she said.

"I know, but we can't exactly tell it that, can we?" I said, getting more and more worried. The oil looked thick and slimy, like glue. "What shall we do?"

Then Reema burst out, "The cape – make a wish."

"Well, I can try," I said. I dashed down to the sea, flung some water on the cape and then whispered fiercely, "I know you're really worn out, but please, Number Seven, I wish you'd use your magic to help this poor seagull in some way. Do this and I won't ask you anything else for ages, I promise."

I tore back up to the beach to Reema and we both stood watching the seagull, waiting for something, *anything* to happen.

But nothing did.

The seagull was still covered in oil and was still desperately trying to clean itself with its beak.

I groaned. "The cape has let us down – *now* what can we do?"

"I don't know," said Reema. "But we can't just leave this poor bird. Oh, it's horrible seeing it like this."

And then a voice said, "You look upset. Can I help?"

We whirled around to see a young woman in jeans and a T-shirt smiling shyly at us. So we pointed at the seagull.

The woman immediately looked angry. "Oh no, there's oil on the beach again." She showed us. "And on the cliffs too. It isn't the first time it's suddenly appeared either."

"But how did it get here?" asked Reema.

"No one's really sure," said the woman. "It could be a ship, I suppose, visiting here at night and then disappearing again before morning. It's a mystery really."

The seagull gave another mournful squawk. "It sounds in such a bad way," said Reema, her voice shaking again. "Is there anything we can do?"

"I'm afraid not," said the woman, "but as it happens, I'm a vet."

Both Reema and I gasped. What an incredibly lucky coincidence. *Or was it?*

"I was supposed to be going to a meeting," the woman went on, "but I found myself taking a stroll along this beach, instead." She gave a puzzled laugh. "Not sure why. Still, it's lucky that I did."

But I soon realized it wasn't luck. It was the magic cape. It hadn't let us down after all.

"The oil's so heavy on its feathers it can't fly or find food," the woman went on. "So I'm going to call a friend of mine at the bird sanctuary."

"What will he do?" asked Reema.

"He'll help me capture the seagull and

then we'll take it to this special cleaning center where they'll flush the oil from its eyes and feathers. Then we'll give the bird some medicine to stop any more damage because of all the oil it's swallowed."

I grinned. "It's funny to think of a seagull sipping medicine."

"I do hope you can save him," said Reema.

"We'll do our very best. My name's Kate, by the way. Here's my card. Do call any time to hear how your bird's getting on."

"Oh, we will," said Reema.

Then we went off and explored the rest of the beach. We had a look in some of the stores too. We were having such fun we forgot all about the time. And when we got back to our little hotel Aunt Nora was waiting for us in the reception area.

"Ah, there you are," she cried. "I was starting to get worried. Have you seen Harry?"

"Happily, no," I said.

But then we *heard* Harry. He was walking into the hotel laughing and chatting with a much older boy.

Harry saw us and yelled, "I just beat Nick here at table tennis."

Nick grinned. "It's true, he did. I was at the sports center down the street looking for someone to play table tennis with when Harry here said he could definitely beat me. And although I think I'm pretty good, he was even better."

I groaned. Harry would be even more big headed now.

"Listen!" Harry shouted.

"Harry, keep your voice down," said Aunt Nora. "Not everyone wants to hear you."

"Don't they?" Harry looked shocked. Then he went on, "Now listen while I introduce you. This is Nick, my new mate, who's also staying at the hotel. Nick, meet my Aunt Nora, and Reema, who's one of my best friends (Reema tried hard not to look too shocked at this) and that's my brother, worse luck, and he's called Jamie. Now, Nick, who would you say was older, Jamie or me?"

"You," Nick said at once.

Harry's face was one big grin now. "I can see why you'd think that, since I'm taller than Jamie and tons better at sports than him. I've won eleven ribbons already, you know, and poor Jamie hasn't won one. But actually I'm *younger* than he is."

It was typical of Harry to show off at my expense. It made my blood boil. In fact, I was so mad I totally forgot my promise not to ask the cape for anything else. Instead, I seized hold of it in my pocket and since it was still a bit wet I whispered, "Number Seven, please turn my brother into the ugliest, most horrible dinosaur in the whole world."

As soon as I'd said it I wished I hadn't. I mean, how was I going to explain a dinosaur suddenly rampaging around the hotel?

But Harry didn't turn into a dinosaur. Instead, he just vanished. Reema looked questioningly at me. And Nick cried, "Where did he go?" But then he grinned. "Oh, there he is, but *look* at him!"

Harry still looked like himself, only now he was snorting around on the carpet on his hands and knees.

Aunt Nora rushed over. "Harry, whatever are you doing? Get up at once!"

Harry just gave a loud grunt in reply.

"What did you say?" asked Aunt Nora.

Harry gave another grunt, which sounded just like a very loud burp. Then, still on his hands and knees, he went lolloping around the reception area.

I stifled a giggle. I guessed the cape didn't have enough magic to change Harry into a dinosaur – so instead it got him to act like one.

A small crowd had now gathered. Harry shuffled over to them, letting out deep cries and squeals. Everyone thought he was just messing around, and started laughing. Especially one man who had the strangest teeth I'd ever seen – they were very large and very black. He put back his head and roared with delight.

Everyone was smiling except Aunt Nora, who was looking more and more flustered.

"That's enough, Jamie," Reema whispered to me. "Turn Harry back now."

So I asked the cape to return Harry to his normal, totally annoying self again. And a few seconds later Harry scrambled to his feet and then blinked around him in astonishment. "What's going on?"

Aunt Nora shook her head. "Just look at you, all covered in dirt. And the little display you put on just now wasn't very funny, you know."

"But what did I do?" asked Harry, looking so bewildered everyone started laughing again.

"Oh," I said, "you only raced around the carpet on your hands and knees making silly noises. Just a normal day's activities for you really."

4. A Scream in the Night

Later I told Harry that I'd tried to turn him into a dinosaur. And he was furious. I can't think why. I thought it was a big improvement.

"You talked so much better when you were a dinosaur," I said.

"But I only grunted," said Harry.

"Exactly," I laughed.

But Harry didn't smile back.

"You're the worst brother in the whole world," said Harry.

"No, I'm not. You're the one who's always showing off about how you're taller than me and . . ."

"Be quiet!" bellowed Harry.

Just then Aunt Nora rushed into our room and for once she looked very angry. "Harry, I can hear you all the way down the corridor. And after your silly behavior earlier today as well, I'm very disappointed in you."

Harry hung his head.

"When I speak to your parents later I don't want to have to say how badly behaved you've been."

Harry hung his head even lower. "No, don't do that, Aunt Nora, please."

"Well, we'll see," she said. "But I want you to be on your best behavior from now on."

As soon as Aunt Nora had gone Harry hissed, "I hate you so much, Jamie, you and your silly cape." Then he added, "Nick's challenged me to another game of table tennis tomorrow. He and I are becoming really good mates."

That evening in the dining room, Nick brought his mom, Mrs. Jones, over to our table.

"Nick's told me all about you," she said. "He can't believe you beat him at table tennis. Not many have managed that, you know."

Mrs. Jones was wearing a great big necklace around her neck and very glittery earrings. In fact, the earrings were glittering so much I couldn't stop looking at them. She smiled at me.

"And what's your name?"

"Oh, he's no one," murmured Harry.

"I'm Jamie," I said.

She nodded and said, "You like my earrings?"

Embarrassed that she'd noticed me looking at her, I muttered, "It's just they really stand out." Then I added, "They must have cost a lot of money."

I don't know why I said that. And I was worried Mrs. Jones would think I was rude.

But she and Nick both just laughed and she whispered, "Don't tell anyone, but they *were* quite expensive, yes."

I giggled nervously, and then Reema nudged me. The man we'd seen earlier with the huge black teeth was leaning forward at his table listening to every word Mrs. Jones was saying.

"Talk about nosy," said Reema.

Later the man came over. "Just had to say 'hello' to this funny lad," he said, smiling at Harry, "and his family, of course.

My name's Luck – Justin Luck." His giant teeth whistled every time he spoke. And his Scottish accent was really exaggerated.

When he'd left, Reema said to me, "I think he's just pretending to be Scottish."

"So do I."

"But why?" she asked.

"I haven't a clue. But there's something really weird about him all right."

After dinner Reema and I called Kate.

"How's our seagull doing?" asked Reema anxiously, holding out the phone so both of us could listen.

"Well," replied Kate, "the oil has been removed."

"Oh, great," Reema and I said together.

"And the bird is now resting in a dark box."

"I bet he hates that," I said.

"No, he's quite calm," said Kate. "We're keeping him nice and warm and he's just enjoyed some chopped-up fish. He's still very weak, but we're keeping our fingers firmly crossed for him."

"And so are we," cried Reema.

Later that night, I couldn't sleep. This was partly because Harry was snoring so loudly, but also because I was thinking about the mystery of the oil on the beach. Would it appear again tonight – making the beach even more dangerous for the poor birds tomorrow? And what was causing it? Was it made by a ship? A phantom ship which only visited the beach at night?

I decided to find out. I shot out of bed. I was going to creep out of the hotel and keep watch on the beach.

I quickly got dressed, and of course, I took my cape with me. I'd just closed the door when suddenly I stopped and jumped in the air with shock.

Someone was screaming.

5. A Suspect

Then I heard a second scream, even louder than the first. It was coming from a room close by. Someone was in trouble. I charged down the corridor, then stopped. On the carpet was a key. Where had it come from? I picked up the key, just as a door burst open.

And there was Mrs. Jones.

"What's wrong?" I asked, rushing over.

But she was staring at the key in my hand. "Where did you get that?" she demanded, a bit rudely, I thought.

"Oh, I just found it," I said.

"Well, I think it might be mine," she said.

She took the key from me just as Nick bounded out of the room next to hers. He still looked half-asleep.

"Mom, what's happened?"

"Oh, Nick," she cried. "I woke up to see this shape moving around in my room. The shock made me scream. And so he ran off. But I think he's taken my lovely earrings."

Then Nick noticed the key in her hand. "Is that the key that went missing from your handbag earlier today?"

"Yes, I think so," she said. "This boy here said he found it."

"It was on the carpet, just outside your door," I said. Nick and his mom gave me an odd look. "Shall I go and get someone?" I asked.

But more doors opened and I didn't need to. Soon everyone was charging around in their bathrobes.

Everyone, except Mr. Luck. Apart from me, he was the only person fully dressed.

"Oh dear me, I thought I heard someone screaming. Whatever's wrong?" he asked in his funny Scottish accent.

I watched Mr. Luck and thought, *You're acting so suspiciously, I wouldn't be surprised if* you've *stolen those earrings.*

But the disturbance didn't wake up Aunt Nora or, more surprisingly, Reema and Harry. I think the sea air had tired them out. So in the end I just slunk back to bed. I suddenly felt too tired to watch for any mysterious ships, and I fell asleep almost at once.

I was woken up by a loud banging. Harry jumped out of bed and opened the door. Aunt Nora was standing there with Nick's mom and a man I dimly recognized as the hotel manager.

Aunt Nora was frowning and saying, "I'm not at all happy about this, boys, but the manager wants to search your room."

6. Harry the Detective

"You want to search our room, oh, excellent. I've never had my room searched before!" said Harry, dancing around excitedly. "I'm actually a detective, so I can help if you like."

"No, thank you," said the manager firmly as he opened the closet and checked inside. I knew he wouldn't find anything, but I still felt hot with anxiety. This was horrid.

"What are you looking for?" asked Harry.

The manager didn't answer, he just went on prowling around our room.

Then Reema rushed in. "What on earth's going on?" she demanded.

"We're having our room searched," said Harry eagerly. "And it's great fun so far."

"Be quiet, Harry," I whispered.

Then Aunt Nora said very softly, "Mrs. Jones had her lovely earrings stolen last night. She didn't see who did it, but she did find Jamie standing outside her door fully dressed. And he was holding a key which earlier had been stolen from her handbag."

"But I can explain all that," I said. "I found the key on the carpet . . . and I was fully dressed because . . ." But if I told Aunt Nora I'd been planning to go on the beach in the middle of the night I'd be in even more trouble. So I quickly tried to think of another reason why I was wandering around at that time. "Oh, I was just . . . just going for a little walk," I said at last, which sounded so unconvincing that I turned my head away from everyone. What a mess!

Then Harry suddenly and very unexpectedly cried out, "I'll tell you one thing about my brother – he's got lots of faults, but he's not a thief."

"No, he isn't," agreed Reema and Aunt Nora together.

I gave them a small, grateful smile. And I was amazed to hear Harry sticking up for me. Then the manager rubbed his hands together and said, "Well, thank you for allowing me to check your room, and sorry for disturbing you."

"That's all right," said Harry. "Just don't do it again."

"I hope you see now," said Aunt Nora to Nick's mom, "that Jamie was certainly not your thief."

But Mrs. Jones didn't answer. She just

gave me a suspicious stare and walked out.

A shiver ran through me. It's horrible being accused of something because even when you're innocent, somehow you still feel so guilty.

Aunt Nora shook her head wearily. "Oh dear, what a thing to happen – perhaps I'm getting too old to look after you all."

"No way," cried Reema. "I think you're wonderful!"

"Thank you, dear," said Aunt Nora.

"And this is just a little misunderstanding," Reema went on.

"Yes, you're right," said Aunt Nora. "I'll go and have another word with Mrs. Jones. I'm sure everything's going to be just fine," she added brightly. "Now I'll see you children downstairs. We'll have breakfast and then, well, I think Harry's off to the sports center with Nick, so maybe we'll go to the swimming pool. Anyway, we'll have a lovely day." She beamed at Reema. "You're right, dear, it's just a little misunderstanding."

After Aunt Nora had gone I told Reema and Harry all about last night. When I mentioned Mr. Luck, Harry burst out, "I bet he's the one who stole those earrings, but everyone suspects you, Jamie."

"No, they don't," I said.

"Yes, they do. You even look guilty. But don't worry," said Harry, picking up his magnifying glass, "you've got the world's greatest detective on your side. Me! And I'm going to start investigating things right now. So you might at least thank me."

"Let's see what you do first," I said.

"Don't worry, I'll have the whole case solved very soon!" announced Harry.

Then he rushed out. Reema laughed. "Who knows what's going to happen now."

I spent most of the morning with Aunt Nora and Reema at the swimming pool. Then we strolled back to the hotel. At once Harry rushed over to Reema and me.

"I've got something to tell you two," he said in the loudest whisper you've ever heard. "After I beat Nick at table tennis again, I talked to him about the robbery. He doesn't think you stole the earrings. But after what happened last night, his mom wants to put her valuable necklace in a safe. Only this hotel hasn't got one. So instead, she's had to leave it in the office. And guess who I just saw standing outside the office door?"

Before Reema and I could reply, Harry hissed, "Mr. Luck. He's planning to steal that necklace. I'm sure of it."

"Look," whispered Reema.

Mr. Luck was walking off to the lounge.

"Follow him," urged Harry.

All three of us bundled into the lounge.

Mr. Luck looked up, saw us, smiled vaguely and then settled down in the corner with two newspapers.

"I'm going to question him," said Harry. Then he plastered a fake beard onto his face.

Reema giggled. "What are you putting that on for?" I demanded.

"He won't be expecting to see a boy with a beard, will he? And he'll be so totally shocked he won't know what he's saying. He might even confess."

I shook my head doubtfully, but Harry dived down next to Mr. Luck and leaned forward. "I'm a detective . . ." he began. Then his beard fell off.

Mr. Luck put down his paper. "What did you say, lad?"

Harry was scrambling around on the ground retrieving his beard. He bobbed up, and waving his beard in one hand and his magnifying glass in the other he announced, "Hi, I'm a detective, and I'd like to ask you a few questions."

"All right," muttered Mr. Luck.

A few minutes later Harry left Mr. Luck and beckoned for us to follow him outside.

"Well, he's clever," said Harry. "Claimed he was fully dressed because he hadn't yet gone to bed – a likely story. But I'll tell you something – that Scottish accent is fake. And his teeth are as real as my beard."

"But no one would have false teeth as ugly as that," I said.

"He's obviously disguising himself so the police don't recognize him. He's probably a famous jewel thief," said Harry. "But don't worry, I'll unmask him very soon." Then he scurried off again.

"At least he's trying to help," said Reema.

"Yeah, but he's still a pain," I said.

Aunt Nora was doing her bit to help me too. She'd gone off to tell the manager she was certain I hadn't stolen the earrings. "I know you very well, Jamie," she said.

"You'd never do anything like that. And it can't be very nice, having this suspicion hanging over you."

"No, it isn't," I agreed.

Aunt Nora bustled off, then Reema and I called Kate again.

"Your seagull ate a good breakfast," she told us. "And has also taken his medicine."

"So he's going to be OK?" asked Reema.

"I think so," said Kate slowly. "It's still early days, though."

After that Reema and I slipped off to the beach, just to check that no other birds had been covered with oil.

Overnight, the air had turned very warm and a beautiful, blue sky bloomed over everyone. The beach was filling up with people too. Yet Reema and I didn't see any of them. We were too busy studying the seabirds. Happily, they all seemed healthy enough. But as we came away from the cliffs I spotted a streak of oil on my shoes.

"The sea is full of oil again," said Reema angrily.

"Tonight I'm definitely going to watch and find out what ship's doing this – and why."

"Only this time I'm coming too," said Reema.

As we walked back to the hotel I suddenly blurted out, "I hate how Nick and his mom think I'm a thief."

Reema gave my hand a squeeze. "I'm sure they'll find the real crook soon."

"And I do have the great detective Harry on the case!"

We both laughed.

But later, when I was alone in my room, I took out my cape. "I know you're on vacation," I whispered, "but I urgently need your help." Then I squirted some water onto it and said, "Number Seven, please grant me this one wish. Let me find out who actually stole those earrings. And don't leave it too long. Thank you very much." Then I gave my cape a little pat. "I know you won't let me down."

7. An Important Discovery

Then I waited for something to happen.

Only nothing did.

Harry said, "I'm watching Mr. Luck all the time. It's really tiring."

"But do you have any clues yet?" I asked impatiently.

"Not yet," admitted Harry.

Later, in the dining room, Nick gave me a little smile, but his mom was very frosty.

We were on our way back to our room when Harry suddenly yelled, "Hey, look!" Outside our door was an envelope. Harry snatched it up. "Oh, it's got your name on it, Jamie. Can I open it for you?" he asked eagerly.

"No, I'll open it myself, thank you," I said, grabbing the envelope from him.

"But how strange that someone's left you a letter like this," murmured Aunt Nora.

She, Reema and Harry waited impatiently while I stared at the scrap of paper. On it was written in huge capitals: I KNOW YOU ARE INNOCENT. SO DON'T WORRY. EVERYTHING WILL BE ALL RIGHT. It wasn't signed.

I read the letter three times. It really cheered me up and I wondered if the cape's magic was starting to work at last. Then I let the others read it.

"But who is it from?" asked Aunt Nora.

"Nick," said Harry at once. "He wants to help you because Nick and I are best mates now."

"Actually I think it's from Nick too," I murmured.

"How jolly decent of him," said Aunt Nora. She smiled at me. "And I think everything's going to be all right as well, so stop worrying, Jamie. Now try and get a good night's sleep."

But of course I wouldn't be sleeping much tonight since Reema and I were sneaking out to discover where all that oil on the beach was coming from. And at exactly midnight, Reema tapped on my door. I quickly slipped on a pullover and jeans and checked I had my cape with me.

Harry was snoring even louder than usual. I was glad about that since I didn't want him tagging along. He'd only get in the way. I stared at him. His snores were really deafening. Lucky I was going out. Then quietly I left the room.

Reema was waiting impatiently in the corridor. "Wouldn't it be funny if someone started screaming again tonight?" she whispered.

"It wouldn't be funny at all," I whispered back. "And let's forget about that now."

We sped down the flight of stairs and into the reception area. No one was around. The chain was on the door. I quickly slipped it off and opened the door.

"Ssh," said Reema.

"I can't be any quieter," I hissed back. But we both held our breath, expecting someone to suddenly appear and demand to know what we were doing. Luckily no one did.

Outside, everything was very still. Nothing stirred except the sea, which made friendly, lapping noises as if murmuring in its sleep. The moon made everything look silvery and mysterious too. And it was amazing having the beach to ourselves.

Neither Reema nor I felt tired. We ran to the cliffs, and then clambered up the side. Soon we were so high up it almost felt like we were flying. And a light gray mist had gathered over the sea making it look quite eerie.

Then I pointed. "Hey, look!"

Far out to sea I could just make out not a ship . . . but an oil tanker. But it wasn't very clear. "We've got to be able to see more," I said.

"Could your cape help?" asked Reema.

I pulled it out of my pocket, dabbed it with water and said, "Number Seven, sorry to bother you again on your vacation, but this is another emergency. Please give Reema and me amazing eyesight for about two minutes."

We waited anxiously and then all at once we could easily see the tanker. We could even make out a man standing on board. Then we noticed something else. All around the tanker a thick blackness filled the water.

"Do you see what's happening?" cried Reema angrily. "That tanker's waited until it's late at night, so no one's around. And now it's washing out all its tanks into the sea. It doesn't care what that's doing to all the birds and animals."

"Look – the tanker has a number," I said. "If we write it down, we can tell Kate tomorrow."

"Great idea," said Reema. "But I don't have any paper or a pen."

And neither did I.

So once again I turned to my magic cape. "Please do this last thing for us," I said.

And just a few seconds later, there on the cliff, nestling among the rocks, was a notebook and pen.

I gave the cape a little pat. "Thanks so much. I promise I won't bother you again tonight."

But in less than an hour, we would urgently need the cape's help.

8. More Shocks

"Well," I said, "we may as well go back to the hotel. We've solved the mystery of the oil on the beach, haven't we?"

"We certainly have," said Reema.

We ran back to the hotel. Then we opened the front door very cautiously and slipped inside.

"Now we've just got to get upstairs," said Reema. "I'm sorry this is nearly over."

But then I saw one of the shadows by the kitchen move.

"Someone else is down here," I whispered.

"Who?" she squeaked.

"Me," replied a familiar voice. "You two didn't half make a racket coming in," he added. Then Harry tiptoed toward us.

"What are *you* doing down here?" I asked.

Harry grinned. "Oh, I only pretended to be asleep. Really convincing, wasn't I? I heard you go outside and guessed you and Reema were going to see who was putting oil on the beach. But I had a special mission of my own. I was watching Mr. Luck's room. And just a few minutes ago he sneaked out and went down to the kitchen." He nodded. "He's in there now."

"What's he doing?" asked Reema.

"Well, it's pretty near the office where that necklace is being kept, isn't it? So I guess he's waiting to strike."

"What's he waiting for?" I asked.

"His accomplice?" suggested Reema.

"Maybe," agreed Harry. "But anyway, you two can clear off up to bed. Leave this to me. I'll work out what's going on." He pulled out his magnifying glass and stole back into the shadows. We followed him.

"Why are you still here?" asked Harry. "You'll ruin everything."

"Look, you can't order us around . . ." I began.

Then Reema hissed, "Don't even breathe – look."

A crouched figure was trying the door handle of the office.

"But how did Mr. Luck get past us?" asked Harry. Then the figure turned around. And it wasn't Mr. Luck at all – it was Nick.

"He must have come to stand guard on the necklace," said Harry at once.

"Ssh," I snapped.

"Don't tell me to ssh," whispered Harry. "I'm a detective."

Then someone else crept forward. It was Nick's mom.

We heard her whisper, "This lock should be easy to open — three or four minutes at the most."

Reema let out a gasp right in my ear.

"Now I want you to keep a lookout, Nick," Mrs. Jones went on. "All right?"

"All right," replied Nick. But he didn't sound very keen.

"Come on now," said his mom softly.

"I don't get why they're doing this," said Reema.

"Neither do I . . ." I began.

And then, before I could say anything else, I felt a hand on my shoulder and a voice whispered, "Don't move."

9. Mr. Luck Tells All

I shot around. There in front of us was Mr. Luck. We all gulped with shock. He looked completely different. Those hideous black teeth had vanished for starters.

"We mustn't talk here. Come into the kitchen," he whispered. "And quickly, please." Mr. Luck's Scottish accent had also disappeared. It was all very weird, but we followed him into the kitchen.

"So come on, what are you up to?" Harry demanded.

"A fair question," said Mr. Luck. "But please keep your voices down. I am, in fact, a private detective. Here's my card."

We all peered at it in the dim light. Right at the bottom underneath his phone number and email address was written:

JUSTIN LUCK
PRIVATE DETECTIVE

"I must get some cards printed soon," said Harry. "I'm a top detective too, you know."

We ignored this and I asked, "Are you here on a case?"

"Yes, my very first one. I'm watching Mrs. Jones and her son, Nick."

"But why?" Harry, Reema and I all asked together.

Mr. Luck raised a hand. "Please, just whisper."

"Sorry," said Reema.

Then he hissed, "Recently Mrs. Jones has been staying at a number of hotels along the coast. At each one she makes sure everyone sees her expensive jewelry. Then she pretends it has been stolen."

"*Pretends!*" echoed Harry.

"Yes, so then she can claim the insurance money. She picks her hotels carefully too — small ones that often don't have a real safe to keep her jewels in. But the insurance company has gotten suspicious."

"And they've asked you to watch her," I said.

"Exactly," said Mr. Luck. "I want to catch her actually breaking into the office — and that should be any moment now."

"And Nick is in on this too?" asked Harry.

"Yes, but very reluctantly, I think," said Mr. Luck. "By the way, did you get my note, Jamie?"

"So it was from you — yeah, I did, thanks."

"You looked so miserable I wanted to let you know that I was on the case."

"As well as me," muttered Harry. Then he

added, "Only I thought *you* were the thief, Mr. Luck. It was your false teeth that did it."

"You didn't like them?" said Mr. Luck.

"No, they're gross. I'd lose them on your next case," said Harry. "And your Scottish accent needs a lot of work."

"Be quiet, Harry," I said.

"No, thanks for the tips," said Mr. Luck, but he looked more than a little crestfallen. "By the way, why are you all roaming around the hotel at this time of night?"

"Well, I was following you, actually," said Harry.

"And we've just been out," I said, "on a supersecret mission of our own – helping to save seabirds."

"You must tell me about it," said Mr. Luck, pushing open the kitchen door a little.

"But not right now . . . they've just gotten inside the office, so it's time for me to act. And I must ask you to leave everything to me."

"Oh, all right," Harry said, disappointed. "Good luck."

"Thanks," said Mr. Luck. Then we watched him speed out and go inside the office.

Nick's mom was crouched down beside the desk trying to pick the lock with her nail file. She had a small flashlight in her other hand.

"Good evening, Mrs. Jones," said Mr. Luck. "Would you mind stepping outside with me, please?"

Mrs. Jones looked around wildly. "I heard a noise downstairs," she started babbling.

"Then I found that the office had been broken into. I just came to check if my necklace was OK."

"It's no good," said Mr. Luck, in a very calm, polite voice. "I've been watching you for some time. Now please follow me." He walked out of the office. "You see, Mrs. Jasper, I am in fact a . . ."

But he didn't get a chance to say another word. A shadowy figure had stolen forward and with one blow sent Mr. Luck tumbling to the ground.

10. Superstrong Jamie

It had all happened so quickly I couldn't even shout out a warning.

Then a voice muttered, "I didn't mean to hit him so hard."

It was Nick.

"You don't know your own strength," said his mom.

"We've got to do something," Reema whispered to me.

But I was already holding my cape (which luckily was still a bit wet) and whispering, "Number Seven, please make me extremely strong. I know I promised no more wishes . . . but this is a total emergency. Please. You've got to help."

Then with lightning speed I leaped up from my hiding place. Nick and his mom were still gazing down at Mr. Luck. I hurtled off in Nick's direction and in a flash I'd jumped up and seized hold of Nick around his chest.

Nick twisted in shock when he felt this boy tornado. Normally he'd have been able to shrug me off in about two seconds. But the cape hadn't let me down. Suddenly I was amazingly strong.

Nick pushed and shoved, but still he

couldn't make me budge. Nick's mom was gaping in astonishment. "Hurry up and pull that little boy off you," she urged.

"I can't," Nick gasped, growing bright red with embarrassment.

Then Harry came slowly out of the shadows. "I never even suspected you," he said gravely to Nick. "Hold him even tighter, Jamie."

Reema rushed over to Mr. Luck. She called his name very softly and he groaned. "What happened?"

"I'm afraid you got knocked out," said Reema.

"Oh, yes, I remember now," said Mr. Luck.

"But don't worry about anything," said Harry bouncing down beside him. "Nick won't hurt you anymore. I've sorted everything out."

"What!" I scoffed.

"With a little help from my two assistants," admitted Harry.

Mr. Luck struggled to sit up and saw me holding Nick in my incredibly powerful grip.

"How," he asked Harry, "is your brother doing that?"

"Oh, we're just an incredibly strong family," said Harry. "Shall I pull you up, Mr. Luck?"

"No, no, I'm all right," said Mr. Luck hastily. He staggered to his feet, with Harry capering beside him.

Then Harry went and stood in front of Nick. "I really thought you were my mate," he said sadly.

"I still am," muttered Nick.

"No, you framed my brother."

"I didn't want to," said Nick miserably.

"And the key," said Harry. "I suppose you pretended it had been stolen, and then dropped it on the carpet just before the fake burglary."

Nick said softly, "I so hated doing it, didn't I, Mom?"

His mom, who'd flopped down on a chair, nodded slowly. She looked weary and defeated.

"And Mrs. Jones," said Mr. Luck, "do you admit you pretended you'd been robbed to claim the insurance money?"

"I'm not saying anything right now," said Mrs. Jones.

"But I *am* saying something!" cried Nick. "Yes, I admit what we've done – and that it was totally wrong. Will you let me go now, Jamie, please?"

"Yeah, go on, let him go," added Harry.

So I did. Nick stood rubbing his arms. "You might not be very big, Jamie, but I've never met anyone so strong. What a family. So what's your secret?"

I smiled down at my cape. "Ah, that would be telling," I said.

11. A Seagull Returns

It was the last day of our vacation.

Earlier Mr. Luck had rushed into the hotel, looking and sounding very different than when he'd checked in as a guest. He said Mrs. Jones had finally confessed to faking burglaries all along the coast.

"Nick deserves another chance though, doesn't he?" Harry put in suddenly.

"I'm glad you said that, Harry," said

Mr. Luck. "I think he does too."

Then he asked if he could take these three "incredible children" out for a meal as a thank you from the insurance company.

But as we were getting ready for our special lunch, Kate turned up. Thanks to Reema and me, she told us, they'd found the oil tanker that had been polluting the sea at night. She was going to make an example of it and try and stop other tankers polluting the sea. And now that our seagull was fully recovered, the people at the bird sanctuary would be releasing him back onto the beach at midday.

Of course, we all had to go along to see our seagull being set free. We watched it fly up into the air, a bit unsteadily at first, and then it disappeared.

Kate and the others from the bird sanctuary went home, but we stayed on the beach for a while longer.

Suddenly Reema cried, "Look!"

A seagull was circling a little shakily over our heads.

"It's come back!" cried Reema.

Then the bird let out a cry.

"I think it's saying thank you," said Aunt Nora.

"No . . . seagulls are always calling out things," I said.

But the seagull went on spinning above our heads and gave another cry.

"And now it's saying goodbye!" cried Reema.

We saw the seagull shoot right up into the air like a silver arrow. And then it was lost to us in a great billowing cloud of birds.

"He's free again," whispered Reema.

"Thanks to you and Jamie," said Aunt Nora.

"And me," cut in Harry.

"You . . . what did you do?" I asked.

"Now don't start arguing again, Jamie," said Aunt Nora. "Don't forget your brother always believed you were innocent and tried to help you clear your name."

"Yeah, OK," I agreed. Then I whispered, "Thank you, Harry."

"Sorry, can't hear you," said Harry.

"THANK YOU, HARRY!" I shouted.

Harry grinned and started leaping around.

Then Aunt Nora told us we should go to lunch. "You're going to be late for your meal with Mr. Luck," she said, and started to make her own way back to the hotel.

I looked at my watch. It was a simple stroll along the beach to the restaurant, but it would take at least twenty minutes. So when Aunt Nora was out of sight I murmured, "I wonder if the cape could help."

I looked at it. The break had certainly done the cape some good. The gold stars around its sides were bright once more. And the number seven had never shone as it did now. I flicked some seawater on it, and then whispered, "Number Seven, please make Reema, Harry and me run to the restaurant really, really fast."

"What have you wished for?" asked Reema.

"You'll see." I grinned. "Right, let's start running!"

"Oh, I hate running," groaned Harry, but then his face was one big smile as the magic started to work. Suddenly neither his feet nor Reema's nor mine seemed to even touch the sand. We flew across that beach with the wind gusting in our ears.

And we arrived at the restaurant four whole minutes early.

Harry shook his head. "What a vacation," he sighed.

I laughed. "For once, Harry, I totally agree with you – what a vacation!"

PETE JOHNSON

Pete Johnson has been a film extra, a film critic, an English teacher and a journalist. However, his dream was always to be a writer. At the age of ten he wrote a fan letter to Dodie Smith, author of *The Hundred and One Dalmatians*, and they wrote to each other for many years. Dodie Smith was the first person to encourage him to be a writer.

Pete is a best-selling author for children and teenagers, whose books have been translated into over twenty languages.

www.petejohnsonauthor.com